WALES & NORTHERN IRELAND

First published in Great Britain in 2008 by
Young Writers, Remus House, Coltsfoot Drive,
Peterborough, PE2 9JX
Tel (01733) 890066 Fax (01733) 313524

Book Design by Tim Christian

SB ISBN 978-1-84431-804-9

FOREWORD

Young Writers was established in 1990 with the aim of encouraging and nurturing writing skills in young people and giving them the opportunity to see their work in print. By helping them to become more confident and expand their creative skills, we hope our young writers will be encouraged to keep writing as they grow.

Secondary school pupils nationwide have been exercising their minds to create their very own short stories, using no more than fifty words, to be included here in our latest competition *Spark the Imagination*.

The entries we received showed an impressive level of technical skill and imagination, an absorbing look into the eager minds of our future authors.

CONTENTS

THE MINI SAGAS

THE SPELL OF SURPRISE

Isobel opened her spell book disguised as an old dictionary. She heard someone muttering and realised her nephew Oliver was reading the book over her shoulder. 'Oops!' she said, he had become a catwalk model. 'Well, at least he's going to be famous!' she exclaimed with a smile.

Jannat Ahmed (13)

OUTER SPACE

I was in my rocket. I could see little dots, stars. I was going that fast it felt like an intense roller coaster. I tried to slow it down but it was too complicated. I sat down and closed my eyes, waiting for it to end.

Liam Price (13)
BRYNMAWR SCHOOL, BRYNMAWR

THE GAME

The light was gloomy as I walked through the forest.
I turned white as a ghost. Branches whacked me
everywhere. I heard a groan. I ran and fell over
a cross, I was out of the forest. Then I was tapped on
the back.
'1, 2, 3, I got you.'

Shannon Willis (13)
BRYNMAWR SCHOOL, BRYNMAWR

THE GRAVEYARD

Opening the crooked gate, I've stumbled into Hell.
The wind picks up and every noise startles me. I walk
past broken headstones, about 1,000 years old. In the
distance I notice something move. I open my mouth
to scream but nothing. Closing my eyes. Nothing.
Opening my eyes … a cat.

Matthew Collier (13)
BRYNMAWR SCHOOL, BRYNMAWR

THE DIAMOND

The king lost his diamond. A magician stole it.
Heroine, on a quest, looking for the magician. She
lost him. There was a figure, a witch, had a necklace.
Heroine went in the cave, fell in a hole, she was stuck.
She found it and returned it to the king.

Bethan Morgan (13)
BRYNMAWR SCHOOL, BRYNMAWR

THE IMMORTAL

Carmen had been sent to rescue Scarlett. Carmen attacked the immortal man, tied him to a chair and looked for Scarlett. The man wanted Scarlett's eye, to replace his old one. Scarlett was tied down on a table, blood all over her face.
Scarlett has only her left eye now.

Brooke Lewis-Richards (13)
BRYNMAWR SCHOOL, BRYNMAWR

THE ARROW

I'm fighting for my life. Swords flying everywhere and
people dead on the floor. I see it flying like a bird
straight towards me. Will it hit me? Will I move?
It strikes me straight in the eye penetrating my brain.
I've lost the battle - The Battle of Hastings!

Daniel Sherman (13)
BRYNMAWR SCHOOL, BRYNMAWR

THE RUN

My feet were swelling, the sun was gleaming and
I was covered in sweat. I was close to last but I kept
going. Up the drive I ran using all my energy. I was
sprinting as fast as I could knowing I'd have a rest.
I'd completed the cross-country.

Ryan Hughes (13)
BRYNMAWR SCHOOL, BRYNMAWR

JIM AND THE TIN

I was walking down the street with my friend called
Jim, when someone threw a tomato at him. 'Tomatoes
are soft,' he said, with a grin.
'Not this one, it comes in a tin!'
Poor old Jim with a tin in his head went to bed with
a sore head.

Craig Suter (13)
BRYNMAWR SCHOOL, BRYNMAWR

SCARY PLANE

Morning. I wake up. Get ready. I am then in the car.
Leaving my house to go to the airport.
Waiting for the plane I am scared. Getting on the plane
still very scared. Going up in the air, travelling to Spain.
It's the worst moment of my life.

Sarah Cunningham (13)
BRYNMAWR SCHOOL, BRYNMAWR

QUEEN INFERNO

Legendary heroine Inferno who went on the most risky quest ever, to get an ancient diamond ring in the deadly sea. To rescue her brother's freedom from the evil king's dungeon. She was more than shocked when she saw the old sea monster. She fought for her life and succeeded.

Chelsea Brain (13)
BRYNMAWR SCHOOL, BRYNMAWR

THE GRAVEYARD

Something tapped me on the shoulder, 'Peekaboo,
I can see you.'
I looked around, my heart was pounding. Where had
they gone, or were they still there?
I couldn't move. I was stuck! I was surrounded by old
gravestones. I shouted, 'Help me please!'
'Hello Meghan it's me!'

Meghan Bolter (13)
BRYNMAWR SCHOOL, BRYNMAWR

THE DRAGON IN THE CHAMBER

The knight had butterflies in his stomach, the hallways shuddered, the ceiling was crumbling, he could hear a strange snoring. The dragon was asleep, sleeping off the sheep. The dragon rolled onto its stomach. 'Perfect.' He raised his sword and with all his strength cleaved the dragon's head off.

Joshua Rowland (13)
BRYNMAWR SCHOOL, BRYNMAWR

THE SCOTTISH KINGDOM

There was a king called Sacher. He was 25 years old. It was a cold, rainy night. He was travelling from Scotland to Philadelphia to save Princess Elaine. King Sacher finally arrived at the evil, damp, dirty castle. He fought a six-headed dog and rescued the princess as well.

Zak Bevans (13)
BRYNMAWR SCHOOL, BRYNMAWR

SKY HIGH

My breath was taken away. My body went numb, so many things went through my mind. I shot to the floor like a bullet from a gun. My life flashed before my eyes. It felt like years, but was over in seconds. My skydive was over and done with.

Emily Marlin (13)
BRYNMAWR SCHOOL, BRYNMAWR

THE DRAGON SLAYER

Damis was on a mission to slay a dragon called
Elvarg. Elvarg was ravaging an island, until Damis
came along and battled Elvarg to death. Damis drew
out a fierce sword. Damis then plunged it through the
heart of Elvarg, he was finally dead!

Jordan Withers (12)
BRYNMAWR SCHOOL, BRYNMAWR

A DANGEROUS QUEST

Merlin sent Tristan off on a dangerous quest, to slay a terrifying werewolf. Tristan turned around as he dug his sharp fangs into his leg. Tristan plunged his sword into the werewolf's side. The werewolf fell to the floor dead, as Tristan screamed in agony.
Merlin arrived and cured him.

Sophie Larsen (12)
BRYNMAWR SCHOOL, BRYNMAWR

MY DESTINY

I rode towards the sunset and my beautiful hair flew in the wind. I galloped across the top of the mountain, I could hear my pony's feet going fast. Suddenly we had to stop. We came to the end of the mountain. I had to turn around and go home.

Bethan Keech (13)
BRYNMAWR SCHOOL, BRYNMAWR

AFRAID

Sitting down in the pitch-black, tears streaming down her face, blood dripping down her leg, bruises covering her stomach. Alone and afraid. Radios play in the background until … approaching footsteps. Loud raised voices. Petrified, she jumps up, wincing in pain, she hides in the corner, as the door opens.

Cerys Nicholas (13)
BRYNMAWR SCHOOL, BRYNMAWR

REVENGED

A friendly young man, whose life had been unkind to him, became obsessed with revenge. He planned alone all day and night, he finally got it. He waited on corners and killed people who no one would miss. His deadly count came up to a hundred and fifty unfortunate strangers.

Kiri Davies (13)
BRYNMAWR SCHOOL, BRYNMAWR

THE FOGGY NIGHT

Walking down from my mate's house when I saw a strange figure in a field. It was a foggy night, every step I took it got closer and close, then the wind started whirling past me faster than ever. I looked back. Nothing ... The wind went dead.

Connor Edwards (13)
BRYNMAWR SCHOOL, BRYNMAWR

A HAUNTED HOUSE

Some boys went inside a creepy house to see if it was haunted. There were cobwebs as big as trampolines. They walked to a door and it opened. They went in wary, the door slammed. They felt something on their legs. They saw something strange and ran home.

Matthew Kale (13)
BRYNMAWR SCHOOL, BRYNMAWR

THRILLER

A thick white line faced me. Three reds then a green …
go! Adrenaline pumped through my body as the wind
blew through my hair, zooming past other people.
Edging ever closer to the corners. People going fast
and slow. What an experience that was.
I was on the … go-karts.

Rhys Bosley (13)
BRYNMAWR SCHOOL, BRYNMAWR

SCARED

Hunched up in the corner, tears streaming down her face, covered in raw bruises, she heard loud music in the background and loud voices echoed in the distance, but getting louder and closer. The footsteps got louder and louder, she jumped up and hid under her bed, her door opened.

Nina Pickering (13)
BRYNMAWR SCHOOL, BL`AENAU

SIR HENRY'S QUEST

A man, Sir Henry, went on a journey to find a golden cup. He was travelling days when he came across a wizard who helped him. He came to the end of his journey and nearly fell off a bridge, but he slayed the dragon and got the cup!

Ebony Smith (13)
BRYNMAWR SCHOOL, BRYNMAWR

ASSEMBLY

We sat down and started talking. One of the teachers
told us to shush as the head teacher came in.
He started to read out all of the match results about
how we beat Nantyglo 5-1 in football. He told us to
bow our heads for prayer. Our Father.

Jake Reeves (13)
BRYNMAWR SCHOOL, BRYNMAWR

THE JOURNEY

The ride started going around in a circle. I felt nervous.
I wanted to be sick. The ride was spinning upside
down then I felt even more nervous. I thought I was
going to fall. Then the ride stopped. I was so glad
to get off.

Shannon Calver (12)
BRYNMAWR SCHOOL, BRYNMAWR

SPEED

'The ride it's huge.'
'Yeah man,' said Jon.
'I am going on it,' said Jill.
The ride was blinding as we went up to get launched out into space. It was so fast. We all now know why it's called 'Speed'!

Ryan White (12)
BRYNMAWR SCHOOL, BRYNMAWR

STOP CHILD ABUSE

He hit the boy with his fist. The boy cried, tears streaming down his face. The man grabbed him by the hair. 'Get me some money tomorrow,' he growled. He tossed the boy into a small, dark room, locking the door. The boy cried, scared and lost in the dark …

Regine Tse (12)
BRYNMAWR SCHOOL, BRYNMAWR

THE HOLIDAY

I took off on the plane, it started bouncing up and
down, I was scared. We were in the air. The plane
turned so it was on its side.
We were heading back for the runway. Suddenly we hit
it. I was safe! We were all safe!

Aaron Rees (12)
BRYNMAWR SCHOOL, BRYNMAWR

MY AUNTIE AND HER BABY BUMP

My auntie is having a baby, we want to know what it is.
She decides to find out. At the hospital the cold jelly
gets put on her tummy – the baby is kicking.
The scanner moves across her tummy.
'It's a boy!' she shouts. 'What shall we call him?'
'Harry!'

Rebecca Howells (12)
BRYNMAWR SCHOOL, BRYNMAWR

TAKE-OFF

As the countdown ended there was a big loud roaring
sound, then a sudden rumbling. People gathered to
watch this amazing event, racing through the air, up,
up, out of the sky, shooting past the clouds.
Now I know what it feels like … to be in outer space!

Jasmine Burns (12)
BRYNMAWR SCHOOL, BRYNMAWR

UNTITLED

I was pitched in the top of an aeroplane, I had my dad
of course, but as I jumped out, I could feel the clouds
hitting me and my skin felt like it was being sucked off
from the wind, but nothing could prepare me for this
… the parachute ripped.

Gavin Seward (12)
BRYNMAWR SCHOOL, BRYNMAWR

SPEED

My heart was pounding as I sat in the seat, I looked
around at the people. They looked as scared as
I did. Without any notice, any signal, it started up and
up and up it went, being thrown side to side, my hair
flowing behind me in the wind.

Katie Thompson (12)
BRYNMAWR SCHOOL, BRYNMAWR

THE THING IN THE DARK

I closed my eyes. I tried to move but my legs wouldn't obey, tried to scream but no sound came. The smell of foul breath got stronger and stronger, the sound of groaning as it raised its hands. I opened my eyes and breathed. The thing in the dark disappeared.

Jessica Capper (12)
BRYNMAWR SCHOOL, BRYNMAWR

OH MY!

Oh great! We're on the top, we are shivering in our boots. Oh no! We are moving girls, we scream. Going down from a big height, oh my, we go upside down, tilted. Oh thank God, it's stopped. The girls look pale and feel sick so do I. Ha ha!

Zoe Leonard (12)
BRYNMAWR SCHOOL, BRYNMAWR

MY JOURNEY TO THE ZOO

We were driving through the zoo when a monkey
jumped on our car and broke the aerial. Father got out
to fix our car, his jeans fell down. My father was angry.
We knew it was the monkey. We went home. The
monkey was in the back of the car.

Charlotte Baldwin (12)
BRYNMAWR SCHOOL, BRYNMAWR

THE ROOM

In Year 6 on a trip to Hilston Park, there was a room at the end of the hall with a woman's picture on it. After Sir left the room and locked the door, we took our torches to investigate. The handle turned, we turned, we ran! *Argh!*

Callum Roberts (12)
BRYNMAWR SCHOOL, BRYNMAWR

THE FLYING THING

I was five years old. I was on this big flying thing. I was scared. It was like I was flying in the air. I was with lots of people.
I could hear voices behind me and the odd baby screaming. It was loud …
Dad said, 'We're off the aeroplane.'

Jake Williams (12)
BRYNMAWR SCHOOL, BRYNMAWR

AVALANCHE

I felt cold going down gathering speed. As I went down I was getting faster and faster, then there was a roaring sound from behind. I looked behind me and slipped. I got up and went faster downwards in a cave, watching the snow slip down. I was safe.

Carwyn Greaves (11)
BRYNMAWR SCHOOL, BRYNMAWR

THE JOURNEY

The children were running on their way home from school, they thought they heard something. They turned around and there were two men. The children hid behind a gravestone and started to run away. They were getting closer and closer. Soon they were safe out of the graveyard.

Ieuan Hughes (12)
BRYNMAWR SCHOOL, BRYNMAWR

THE BIG BANG!

3, 2, 1! Blast-off! A big bang, I shot up through the sky.
I couldn't breathe. All was silent. I was in space! We
took off our belts and floated like birds. An alarm went!
I jumped into my seat. We dropped through the sky.
What a great experience.

Brendan Elliott (12)
BRYNMAWR SCHOOL, BRYNMAWR

A DARK STREET IN THE EAST END

I'm alone. I'm walking down a narrow street at dusk.
I shouldn't be here. It's too dangerous. I didn't see
the knife coming. I only felt it, with pain too great to
imagine. I'm lying here, blood flowing from my wound.
I think I'm going to die. God save me!

Sam Thorp (12)
CAEREINION HIGH SCHOOL, WELSHPOOL

THE END OF THE WORLD

Tom woke up one quiet morning and to his amazement the streets outside were bare – no vehicles, people, animals – nothing but flames and dismantled buildings. He turned on the television but there was no signal. The phone and radio weren't working either. There was no one left but him.

Aled Evans (14)
CAEREINION HIGH SCHOOL, WELSHPOOL

THE GRAND SLAM

I was running vigorously, my heart beating. I had so much adrenaline running through me. Yes! Only one opponent to get past. I could feel him biting at my heels. I managed to get through the gap between the energy players and yes! I'd scored the winning try for England.

George Fox (12)
CAEREINION HIGH SCHOOL, WELSHPOOL

EXECUTION

The yells of the crowd screamed for blood which I was sure would not be denied. I said my final prayer to God and placed my head upon the block, the blood of its previous victim warm against my trembling neck. Silence was hailed and the great blade fell again.

Owen Farrington (15)
CAEREINION HIGH SCHOOL, WELSHPOOL

MY BIG GAME

My hands are shaking, my knees quivering. I'm in the final at Wimbledon. My opponent is the toughest yet, we are both at match point. The crowd is cheering and clapping. This is my big chance. My arm stretches higher than it ever has before. Game, set, match, I've won!

Amy Williams (14)
CAEREINION HIGH SCHOOL, WELSHPOOL

WAS IT THE END?

The radio crackled and the family waited eagerly to hear the news. Dorothy's husband had gone to war. As she played with her hair in her sweaty palms, she paused nervously. There was a news flash. No name so far. The radio ceased. Dorothy was anxious. Was it the end ... ?

Charlotte Smith (14)
CAEREINION HIGH SCHOOL, WELSHPOOL

THE HOUSE ON THE LAKE

There was once a house on a small island in the middle of a stagnant lake. For a thousand years it had lit up a dark crimson-red. A boy had died there at dawn. To this day people still see a small child swimming in the lake.

Hedd-Wyn Richardson (13)
CAEREINION HIGH SCHOOL, WELSHPOOL

FROM ABOVE

I looked up to see it coming towards me, an aeroplane! I started running, moving as fast as a cheetah. The turbines were just a metre away. I dived to the floor as the plane flew over, shredding my rucksack in the propellers.

Joe Richings (14)
CAEREINION HIGH SCHOOL, WELSHPOOL

AN UNWANTED VISITOR

The Mercedes drove up to the building, brakes squealing in hesitation. He breathed in deeply, stroked his silk pocket and walked from the car into the night. Looking around to check he wasn't being followed, he crept towards the abandoned home. Suddenly shockwaves rippled through his body.
They had waited.

James Sutherland (14)
CAEREINION HIGH SCHOOL, WELSHPOOL

BLACK DOG

I was walking up a mountain when suddenly I saw two
yellow glaring eyes, and then smelled *blood.* It went all
foggy and an unnatural cold came over me.
As I stepped back it continued walking towards me.
Then, my torch went out. It pounced, I fell, it ate me.

Adam Pincombe (14)
RADYR COMPREHENSIVE SCHOOL, CARDIFF

THE CAR

Finally the day had come. The day that had been promised to me for years. My dad's car pulled up outside the car dealership. I was so excited I didn't sleep the night before. Just imagine me driving away in my brand new car. I entered the dealership high-hoped.

Kim Newberry (14)
ST COLUMBANUS' COLLEGE, BANGOR

IN THE DARK

I hate the dark, I always have. It's as if as soon as that sun goes down or light flicks off a whole different place is around me, a place where nothing is certain of who or what is near …

Kate Keenan (14)
ST COLUMBANUS' COLLEGE, BANGOR

NEW BEGINNING

He was lying there, his cold cheeks turning blue,
lips that were purple. But he couldn't feel my hands
upon his golden hair. My fingers crawling though his
adorable curly locks. Remembering how he told me he
loved me until the end. But it felt like the beginning.

Hannah Rose (15)
ST COLUMBANUS' COLLEGE, BANGOR

WHERE FISHERS FISH

There I was climbing the rocks on the shore where fishers fish. One wrong step and I was falling, falling. Head swimming, belly tingling. A splash and the sound of laugher.
'We've caught a big one,' the fisherman giggled.

Luke Rainey (14)
ST COLUMBANUS' COLLEGE, BANGOR

THAT'S WHEN I REALISED!

I hear the birds crow, as the black gloomy car strolls down the stony old hill. I hear the sobs and cries of the older members of the crowd. I walk with my dad and realise that she's gone, forever.

Jillian Boyd (14)
ST COLUMBANUS' COLLEGE, BANGOR

THE CHASE

I felt fear and worry as I ran through the forest. He was chasing me, running as fast as he could, I was scared. It was dark and gloomy. I could hear the owls and wolves howling. This was a nightmare, thoughts going through my head and then, I tripped.

Rachel Donaghy (14)
ST COLUMBANUS' COLLEGE, BANGOR

STRIKE

I was anxiously waiting, the pressure was on, one false move and my dreams were over, down came the pins, up went my arm, *whoosh,* the ball went flying. Strike, yes! I'm the winner, the glory went through my head and shot all over my body, I can't believe it.

Connor Lynch (14)
ST COLUMBANUS' COLLEGE, BANGOR

THE BULLY

Another bruised cheek and black eye. I'm so embarrassed. What would they say in school? Laughing. Being jeered at. Even the weirdos will join in. Ha ha, you were beat up by your sister. I have to take the abuse. I can't tell them who it was ...

Ryan Rogan (14)
ST COLUMBANUS' COLLEGE, BANGOR

IN THE DARK

Darkness is everywhere, even when you close your
eyes. It's always around us and can come with a
surprise. You hear little noises from time to time.
How can you sleep without the light on?
Certain things are in the dark. We can't see them but
they can see us.

Jessie Davidson (14)
ST COLUMBANUS' COLLEGE, BANGOR

THE FRIGHTENING GAME

Her heart started thumping. She was so scared. The
lights on the plane went off and it started shaking. She
thought she was going to die. It started going down,
faster and faster then … *crash.*
She was so happy the game was over.
It felt like real life.

Hayley Adair (14)
ST COLUMBANUS' COLLEGE, BANGOR

LATE AGAIN

I am shaking, I feel like I am about to face the firing squad. This is about the fifth time in the past month I have been home late, but this is the latest I have been. I can see Mum's face, the look of disappointment. Here I go.

Carrie Pyper (14)
ST COLUMBANUS' COLLEGE, BANGOR

THE IRISH DANCING COMPETITION

My legs trembled with fear. Nerves struck me as I walked on the stage. I told myself, 'I can do this.' The musicians played, I danced light and free. Was it good enough to win? The results came and I had done it. I had won the Irish dancing competition.

Gemma McGimpsey (14)
ST COLUMBANUS' COLLEGE, BANGOR

SHELLS

The sea hits me, hits me hard. I knock off a rock. I may never be found, sometimes you see me sitting in the sand. What texture am I? Hard, soft or bumpy? Most kids love me. If you pick me up and listen hard you can hear the sea.

Sarah McLoughlin (15)
ST COLUMBANUS' COLLEGE, BANGOR

THE MONSTROSITY OF THE MAD MOUSE

As she and her friends walked through town together, the fair was about to open. They lined up for the mad mouse. It was raining the night before. Four carts, four seats, fourth in line. They got to the front, they went up the slope, people watching anxiously. *Bang!* Sirens.

Ashleigh Crawford (14)
ST COLUMBANUS' COLLEGE, BANGOR

THE FOOTSTEPS

A cold winter night walking along the beach, raindrops
trickling down my face. When walking I tripped on
something. It was a shell, an echo came from it.
The trees rustled helplessly. I looked behind me and
I saw footsteps that did not belong to me.

Ruth Hall (15)
ST COLUMBANUS' COLLEGE, BANGOR

THE PARK

The sun was glistening high in the sky when I was strolling through the park. It was a beautiful day and birds were singing. The children were chattering. All of a sudden I saw a young boy, unhappy, his ball was stuck in a tree so I helped him.

Marcus Hill (14)
ST COLUMBANUS' COLLEGE, BANGOR

WHEN IT ALL FALLS APART

Fear ignited in my veins. I looked around me. Fire
burning. Adults screaming. Children crying.
Why? Hands crept up my arms and I felt breathing at
my neck.
'Time to go,' a man whispered behind me. Grabbing
my hand, he trailed me away as my home crumbled
down around me.

Hazel McKinley (14)
ST COLUMBANUS' COLLEGE, BANGOR

THUNDER AND LIGHTNING

It was a cold dark night. I could hear the rain crashing down and hitting the windows rapidly. I began to hear a loud rumble. I hid under my duvet breathing heavily. The lightning came soon after. I saw the beam of light through my curtains.

Emma Young (14)
ST COLUMBANUS' COLLEGE, BANGOR

IN THE NAVY

I'm in the sea cadets and this year I went on a boat called HMS Bulwark. While on that trip we were shown how to save a man overboard and seamanship, but best of all – getting to know that being in the navy would be the career of a lifetime.

Aimee Davey (14)
ST COLUMBANUS' COLLEGE, BANGOR

FERNANDO THE FROG

Fernando was a frog, a green frog. Fernando longed
to be red. He wanted to be red so much he even
jumped into paint. He got bullied at school.
'Hey greenie,' they shouted. Fernando prayed to God.
God told him that he was special and Fernando knew
he was right.

Ryan Jones (13)
WELSHPOOL HIGH SCHOOL, WELSHPOOL

TED'S EXPLOSION!

Ted was a fat ginger cat. He would eat anything edible.
He ate all day and slept all night. One day, he ate
all of the food in the house. Suddenly, he burst into
thousands of pieces.
'That's what you get for being a fat cat,' said his owner.

Zoë Greenslade (13)
WELSHPOOL HIGH SCHOOL, WELSHPOOL

THE ROOM

The room is getting smaller and smaller, faster and faster. There's no chance of me escaping. I have already given up. My breathing is getting quicker and it is getting harder. I am screaming at the top of my voice even though I know it's hopeless.
Is this the end … ?

Delyth Humphreys (13)
WELSHPOOL HIGH SCHOOL, WELSHPOOL

THE PERFECT FRIEND

'She has to go,' said Dad, holding the knife.
I cried and squealed, clutching her scruffy feathers.
Yesterday, Mum saw me stroking Ginger's featherless,
half bald back. How could anyone spoil the
relationship with my scruffy, 'battered' chicken? To me,
she is the most perfect, best friend ever. My chicken.

Jessica Long (12)
WELSHPOOL HIGH SCHOOL, WELSHPOOL

THE BEE

The bee. The bee … it was following me. After every movement the buzzing was ringing in my ear. I turned. We were face to face. Just me and the bee like in those old cowboy movies. Who will strike first, but in my case who will run? *I* ran. *'Argh!'*

Amy McCudden (13)
WELSHPOOL HIGH SCHOOL, WELSHPOOL

THE BRAIN

Dr Frankenstein felt a rush of excitement as he gazed into the glass tank. The tank was bathed in an eerie light. In the light was a strange pulsating object. 'It's alive!' whispered Dr Frankenstein excitedly.
He was the first person to keep a human brain alive outside the body.

Kieran Barrett (13)
WELSHPOOL HIGH SCHOOL, WELSHPOOL

LARRY

Larry was a goldfish. Larry was lonely. He swam around his bowl, wishing he had a friend. He dreamed every day of having a friend. One day his dream came true in the form of a TV. Every day he watched his beloved TV. Then Larry was no longer lonely!

Sam Leese (13)
WELSHPOOL HIGH SCHOOL, WELSHPOOL

THE TREE'S DISASTER

As the tree's branch broke off, the tree gave out
a scream.
I went and asked him, 'What's the matter?'
The tree replied, 'My branch has broken off in that
evil wind.'
So I got some Pritt Stick out of my pocket and glued
the branch back on.

Rhys Phillips (12)
WELSHPOOL HIGH SCHOOL, WELSHPOOL

DISH OF THE DAY

I couldn't understand why the customers stared at my
masterpiece as though it were a disaster.
'Excuse me, we ordered the meal of the day,' said one,
prodding my work of art gingerly.
'And you got it,' I replied, annoyed. Had they never
seen a jellyfish and kangaroo pizza before?

Jacob Owen (12)
WELSHPOOL HIGH SCHOOL, WELSHPOOL

MY PRINCE CHARMING

I must be dreaming, Ashley thought as she walked down the stairs of the castle. She had found her Prince Charming and he *was* a prince!
Ashley was dancing around all night. She was beautiful. They were perfect for each other but she was so full with excitement she fainted.

Ella Cadwallader (12)
WELSHPOOL HIGH SCHOOL, WELSHPOOL

THE CRAZY MAGICIAN

One day a shortsighted magician called John was conducting an experiment on how to vanish rats. John went to buy some rat detergent. The magician made the experiment then put it on the mousetrap. It blew the mousetrap up and ever since, John hasn't done magic again.

Bethan Davies (12)
WELSHPOOL HIGH SCHOOL, WELSHPOOL

THE WAVING FIGURE

The cellar was cold and wet. Only the creaking in corners made this place feel connected to life. Suddenly a looming figure came from out of the doorway. I screamed. It was coming closer and closer. Its arms were waving threateningly. The light turned on; it was only Dad.

Megan Over (12)
WELSHPOOL HIGH SCHOOL, WELSHPOOL

FISHING TRIP

One day John and I were out fishing. Suddenly a fast flow whooshed down the river and carried John away. I ran, shouting for help but I wasn't heard. He was holding the foot of the bridge. I grabbed a stick and pulled him out. After that, we went home.

Liam Astley (12)
WELSHPOOL HIGH SCHOOL, WELSHPOOL

LEARNING TO SWIM

Bubbles escape from her mouth and rush upwards,
breaking the surface into the sunshine. The murky
water swallows her resolve and the struggling ceases.
The water whispers secrets, slowly sending her to a
dreamless sleep. Sunlight runs from the shadow of a
hand as it pulls her, coughing, ashore.

Daragh Quinn (15)
WELSHPOOL HIGH SCHOOL, WELSHPOOL

THE MOONLIGHT HORSE

Once there was a moonlight horse named Snowflake.
She was special because she could only leave her
palace for a single hour at moonlight. This was
because she was under a curse, and the only way for
the curse to be broken was for her to find her true love.

Shannen Thornton (12)
WELSHPOOL HIGH SCHOOL, WELSHPOOL

BETHAN AND THE GORILLA!

One day Bethan walked out of her door but not into her street, she walked into a jungle. Suddenly a gorilla appeared before her.
She screamed, 'Don't eat me, I have bananas.'
The gorilla ran after them. Bethan ran through the door and arrived at school.

Chloe Aldis (12)
WELSHPOOL HIGH SCHOOL, WELSHPOOL

MY SAILING TRIP

Jim and I went sailing. Jim had never sailed before so
after a while he got bored and fell out of the boat and
floated off. When I got to shore a boat came to me and
Jim was inside.
Jim said, 'I'm never going sailing again.'

William Butler (11)
WELSHPOOL HIGH SCHOOL, WELSHPOOL

SHH, IT'S A SECRET

I sat in the playground, talking to my best friend, when
'he' walked past.
I should tell her, I can trust her, I thought. So I told her,
I told her my big secret.
The next day, 'he' walked past again, laughing at me!
She told him! I was mortified.

Cerys Bennett (13)
WELSHPOOL HIGH SCHOOL, WELSHPOOL

THE BIG MISTAKE

One morning Owen took his dog Fluffy for a walk in the park. 'Oh,' said Owen holding his nose, 'what a smelly mess you've made.' Owen left the mess and walked on. When Owen was returning he slipped in Fluffy's mess. 'Oh,' said Owen, 'I should have cleaned that up.'

Alexandra Fellows (13)
WELSHPOOL HIGH SCHOOL, WELSHPOOL

THE BOX

A box came this morning. It wasn't a big box but it wasn't tiny. I thought it was a present for me. Maybe it was a PlayStation game or a new DVD. I wanted to know what was inside it. It turned out just to be a book for Mum.

Rhys Williams (13)
WELSHPOOL HIGH SCHOOL, WELSHPOOL

MY FROG, CANDY-KING

I was in my garden, by my pond, eating candy until I saw a huge frog ... ! 'Hello,' I said, 'would you like my candy?' I placed it by its mouth and it gobbled it up. 'You're my frog friend, I've decided and I think I will name you ... Candy-King.'

Laura Hudson (13)
WELSHPOOL HIGH SCHOOL, WELSHPOOL

EMBARRASSED

I stood up, gobsmacked. I walked through the crowds and up on to the stage. All the people were staring at me. I had been waiting for this moment all my life, practising my speech. So I said it. Silence. Only then I realised it wasn't my name called out.

Sophie Kumar-Taylor (13)
WELSHPOOL HIGH SCHOOL, WELSHPOOL

THE GIRL WITH PINK HAIR

Lilly had pink hair, her mum had yellow and her dad had red. Everyone made fun of them. Then there was a competition for the freakiest hairdo. The prize; a holiday in Florida. The family won and for the rest of their lives they were respected for who they were.

Sioned Edwards (13)
WELSHPOOL HIGH SCHOOL, WELSHPOOL

ANNABELLE AND HER DOLPHIN DREAM

Annabelle's dream took her to where her favourite animal was. She saw the dolphin and said, 'You're lovely.' When she looked and saw a shark the dolphin jumped over Annabelle and saved Annabelle's life. Annabelle got food for the dolphin. Then the dolphin took Annabelle for a swim.

Kimberley Richards (12)
WELSHPOOL HIGH SCHOOL, WELSHPOOL

BYE-BYE BEAR

One day Jessie was at the beach with Bear. Mum had told Jessie not to take Bear.
'Bear!' shouted Jessie, as she watched him drift further out to sea. 'Bye-bye Bear,' Jessie said as she started to cry.
'It's OK,' said Mum, 'we'll get you another bear.'

Laura Haysell (12)
WELSHPOOL HIGH SCHOOL, WELSHPOOL

SOMETHING FROM OUTER SPACE

One day I was in my room when suddenly I saw a
bright light. Then an alien came from nowhere and
said, 'Do not be afraid, I will not hurt you.'
I didn't know what to do so I ran into the kitchen.
I never saw an alien again!

Christa Humphreys (12)
WELSHPOOL HIGH SCHOOL, WELSHPOOL

THE LOST BOY

One day an Italian boy from Rome was trekking
through a crisp cornfield, the sun blazing and the
beads of sweat sliding down his cheek. As he thrust
his palm over his forehead he suddenly collapsed into
a trap.
As his alarm clock rang his heartbeat had stopped.

Kenneth Villis (12)
WELSHPOOL HIGH SCHOOL, WELSHPOOL

THE CHASE

One day a boy called Simon was biking to the shop
to get some sweets when a dog started chasing him.
He wanted the sweets in his pocket and they were the
dog's favourite. He biked for miles till finally the dog
gave up.
He never brought sweets ever again.

George Mitten (12)
WELSHPOOL HIGH SCHOOL, WELSHPOOL

BURIED ALIVE!

I was lying on the beach one day. I must have fallen asleep because when I woke up I was buried in sand! My brother was looking at me with a cheeky grin on his face! I unburied myself, got a bucket of water and threw it over him!

Poppy Morris (13)
WELSHPOOL HIGH SCHOOL, WELSHPOOL

THE HAT AND THE DUSTBIN

My hat was in the dustbin. It was my lucky hat. I wore it for years and I never took it off. It had colourful explosions and sparkles on it. It was a weird shape but nice. It was in the dustbin. My hat was in the dustbin.

Jack Lewis (13)
WELSHPOOL HIGH SCHOOL, WELSHPOOL

THE MELTDOWN

It is sunny – too sunny. If I'm not careful, my ice cream will melt and drip like big, mint choc raindrops. I look left; my sister's ice cream is perfect, with continuous licks to make it a neat cloud of vanilla … Oops. I look down. Ice cream in my lap.

Lucy Wain (13)
WELSHPOOL HIGH SCHOOL, WELSHPOOL

COMPETITION

One day I entered a competition.
I received a phone call one hour later.
'Congratulations, you have …'
I ran around the room screaming thinking I had won.
The man on the phone finished his sentence, '…
entered the competition.'

Ashley Darrall (13)
WELSHPOOL HIGH SCHOOL, WELSHPOOL

MR E

Yesterday, I found a small grey animal on the pavement. I took him home, fed him grapes and gave him a place to sleep. By this morning, he hadn't moved. I picked him up gently and studied him until my eyes were sore. Now I've realised ... he's a rock!

James Batten (12)
WELSHPOOL HIGH SCHOOL, WELSHPOOL

THE FEATHER

She waited for a sign. Any sign to say, 'It's OK, I'm alright.' One never came. She went to the graveyard every day to see the one she missed. One day, she watched as a pure white feather fell before her. She looked to the sky and smiled. 'Thanks, Mum.'

Jessica Abby Ackerley (14)
YSGOL BRYN ALYN, WREXHAM

MODERN SAVAGERY

Screams echo. The prey stumbles, panting, glasses falling. Knives glint in the dying light and battle cries roar at the dark. The pack moves as a unity, incomprehensible. The leader's eyes glaze over, focuses, dives, delivers the fatal blow. Bloodshed. A mobile phone rings. Rain descends on a broken world.

Cerys May Jones (14)
YSGOL BRYN ALYN, WREXHAM

COLD CONDITIONS

It was cold, freezing in fact. It had gone now, we were alone. I swam to keep warm but it was no use, the cold icy water was overtaking me. I thought I was going to a watery grave but one boat came back, just one boat. Thank you God.

Sebastian Hicks (14)
YSGOL BRYN ALYN, WREXHAM

DEAD WEIGHT!

The boy walked in and found him on the body. He dived on him, the boy fell on the stairs, man behind knife in hand, then into the road. Then he saw the car, horn blared, man just behind, brakes screeched. A dead weight hit the floor. The man vanished.

Tom Williams (14)
YSGOL BRYN ALYN, WREXHAM

THE DEAD OF NIGHT

They were running, sweating, gaining on him. He was panting, gasping for breath, slowing. They hoped he would give up. They ran through the city in the dead of night. He ran until he could run no more. They pounced. A scream. Silence. They didn't know he had a knife!

Alex Hayes (14)
YSGOL BRYN ALYN, WREXHAM

IT WAS THERE

He carried on running away down the street, not looking back. Then he turned around the corner. By now he was out of breath so he stopped and leant on the lamp post. He got his breath back and was about to set off. He turned round, it was there!

Matthew Mault (14)
YSGOL BRYN ALYN, WREXHAM

ANYTHING BUT A CHICKEN

Calls of 'chicken' rang in her ears as the roller coaster climbed higher and higher. The water below her rippled and the loops twisted before her.
'It'll be fine.' The boys next to her were reassuring. She breathed out. As the roller coaster turned upside down, she slipped and fell.

Sadie Morris (13)
YSGOL BRYN ALYN, WREXHAM

THE LONELY OLD MAN

The lonely old man stood alone in the cold outside.
He looked up at the sky and wondered where she
was. He walked into the building with beautiful stained
windows. He sat down in the corner and looked ahead
at the cross. A tear rolled down his old worn face.

Hannah Greenough (14)
YSGOL BRYN ALYN, WREXHAM

INTO THE LIGHT

I woke up in a tunnel, bright light at the end. I pulled myself off the ground and wandered into the light. My sister ran towards me, mascara running down her face. She sat beside a body, weeping. It's only then I realised, the body she's next to was mine.

Emma Roberts (14)
YSGOL BRYN ALYN, WREXHAM

THAT DREAM

'You have a huge responsibility and if you know what
you want, go for it'. She's lived by this phrase all her
life. She knew what she wanted and had worked so
hard for it.
That dream started when she was ten and now she is
old, but without regret.

Cerys Roles (14)
YSGOL BRYN ALYN, WREXHAM

FINAL THREE SECONDS

Down by three points, three seconds left in the game. This one shot will determine everything. His life, his family, his future. The whole arena pauses. His heavy breathing echoes around the stadium. Just one missed trigger will destroy it all. One bounce of a ball. Then it is done.

Ashleigh Davies (14)
YSGOL BRYN ALYN, WREXHAM

NO!

He stands there frozen. They walk closer. He looks,
stares, he wishes. Still they walk closer. He backs
away. 'What have I done?'
They murmur louder and louder. He turns, they punch,
they kick, they laugh. He cries, he's scared, he's
alone. The bullies leave the victim bullied, defeated.

Melissa Siân Jones (14)
YSGOL BRYN ALYN, WREXHAM

WINDING METAL

The winding metal flew in front of me in a blur. Full of excitement but also an unusual fear. The metal seemed to move, the ground, the sky and myself. Time seemed to stand still. My winding destination seemed to have no existence. I know I'm safe, but still fear.

Aaron Williams (14)
YSGOL BRYN ALYN, WREXHAM

QUICK CURRENCY

My heart was in my throat as I went into the bank. I waited in the queue sweating madly. Everyone was looking suspiciously at me. It felt like years. I reached into my pocket as the cashier asked how he could help me. Then I nervously took my gun out.

Ben Rogers (12)
YSGOL GYFUN DEWI SANT, HAVERFORDWEST

THE DENTIST

Time for a check-up again. I hate the dentist. He
scares the life out of me. The big chair and lights and
the way he chuckles.
'Open wide Rebecca.' He grabs the big drill and starts
to poke … I hear a crack. He gasps, 'Oh dear.'
The blood trickles.

Rebecca Deeley (12)
YSGOL GYFUN DEWI SANT, HAVERFORDWEST

DEATH IN THE WATER

Crash! go the waves on the trawler. The wind chilling
and icy, then I am back in the water. Thrashing, bone-
breaking in the blue ocean, flinging me on the current.
Everybody shouts and the death net lifts me up.
I black out. I am on Morrison's fish counter. Dead.

George Harding (12)
YSGOL GYFUN DEWI SANT, HAVERFORDWEST

PLATYPUS-MAN

Aw! Persie got bitten by a platypus with two brains. Persie woke up the next day to discover he had a bill and a furry tail. He was determined to be a superhero. But his platypus instinct caused him to be scared of people, he can't overcome his fears!

Daniel Rees (13)
YSGOL GYFUN Y CYMER RHONDDA, PORTH

STREET RACER

A daring young boy grows up to be his dream, a street racer. At his first competitive illegal race he blitzes everyone, earning respect. Gradually, he has the best name on the streets, before he gets busted by police. Eventually he gets out, left to race the new street king.

Hywel Nathaniel (15)
YSGOL GYFUN Y CYMER RHONDDA, PORTH

THE END OF THE WORLD

They were in the garden when suddenly the wind started roaring. Everything went dark and the shadows gathered in the sky. 'Get the kids in!' They all ran for shelter from the acid rain.
'Those pesky greenflies!' said the man as he turned off his bug exterminator hose.

Sophie Louise Hazell (12)
YSGOL GYFUN Y CYMER RHONDDA, PORTH

THE SWORD IN THE STONE

The first tribe went charging at the castle with the
squelching sound of mud. When they reached the
castle they found nothing at all, only a sword in the
stone. One of them decided to pull this mysterious
sword from the stone and succeeded.
All were amazed.

Luke James Iwan Harris (12)
YSGOL GYFUN Y CYMER RHONDDA, PORTH

UP ABOVE!

In a school far away there were heroes that saved the day. One boy had heroes for parents but he never had magic. Would his powers finally turn up or would his parents save him? Would the evil defeat the good or would he finally save us himself?

Chloé Marianne Tutton (11)
YSGOL GYFUN Y CYMER RHONDDA, PORTH

REVENGE OF THE HEADMASTER

A boy called Jack went to school and got picked on. The bullies stole Jack's dinner money. He told the teacher but she didn't say much. Then Jack told the headmaster. The headmaster had a quiet word with the bullies and warned them. They didn't bully Jack ever again.

Seren Hâf MacMillan (12)
YSGOL GYFUN Y CYMER RHONDDA, PORTH

HITCHHIKER

John stopped to give the man a lift. They drove in silence. Suddenly the hitchhiker shouted, 'Stop! Let me out!' He viciously grabbed John's leg, the car screeched to a halt and the man fled.
Shaking, John looked down and watched in horror as a bloody handprint slowly disappeared.

Alex Morris (13)
YSGOL GYFUN Y CYMER RHONDDA, PORTH

THE MONSTROUS KITTEN

He sprinted to get away from the monster. 'Help! It's after me!' he screamed. People came running from their houses, wondering what the commotion was and what he was screaming about. He turned around and to his amazement the monster he had been running from was a newly born kitten!

Kirsty Toolan (12)
YSGOL GYFUN Y CYMER RHONDDA, PORTH

THE CONSEQUENCE OF GREED ...

'I will strike you down with great anger!' screamed Jules as he shot Tommy Fonteyn. He jumped into his Cadillac and sped off. The police were pursuing him, a shot was fired but who got shot, Jules or the policeman?
Was this really worth the money Jules stole?

Ross Farrup (13)
YSGOL GYFUN Y CYMER RHONDDA, PORTH

A MAN IN A CAGE

The moonlight is shining on me. All alone wanting
to be free. These bars are getting to me, the guards'
footsteps are getting louder. Don't know what to do in
this boxed room. Why did I steal it? Why didn't I listen?
I could be free.

Josh Turner (12)
YSGOL GYFUN Y CYMER RHONDDA, PORTH

EURO 2008

It was the final of the Euro 2008, Spain versus Germany. There was a slight problem for Spain, their three star players were missing. They were Cesc Fabregas, Fernando Torres and David Villa. Suddenly the crowd roared as they arrived. The game was theirs!

Ashley Paul Doggett (12)
YSGOL GYFUN Y CYMER RHONDDA, PORTH

THE APACHE SOLDIER

An Apache soldier gathered his army, they all rode on
horseback two by two, all of them with rifles in
their hands.
They saw the town, they all stopped in one gigantic
line. One man held up his gun and charged, the
soldiers followed him. Only one man survived.

Alex Judd (12)
YSGOL GYFUN Y CYMER RHONDDA, PORTH

THE FINAL

'Scott, pass me the ball,' I screamed to him.
He swiftly passed me the ball. But number four
snatched it from Me. Me and Scott paddled to the
goals as quickly as we could. We both blocked the
goals with our paddles. But sadly we lost the final.

Abbi Morris (13)
YSGOL GYFUN Y CYMER RHONDDA, PORTH

THE THONG

He runs down the line like a lightning bolt! A big fat juicy prop dives and grabs his shorts and pulls them down. Everyone's giggling, he looks down to see a leopard skin thong.
The ref asks, 'Are thongs appropriate for rugby?'
He giggles.

Jay Harris (13)
YSGOL GYFUN Y CYMER RHONDDA, PORTH

CINDERELLA

Cinderella was a slave for her stepmother. They got invited to a ball. Cinderella fell in love with the prince but he loved her stepmother. Cinderella kidnapped her and locked her in the attic.
So Cinderella got to be with the prince and they lived happily ever after.

Lowri Heledd Thomas (13)
YSGOL GYFUN Y CYMER RHONDDA, PORTH

THE BATTLE

It was the first day of the battle, Greeks against the mighty Persians. The battle began. There was blood everywhere, over the horses and men, it was brutal. Thousands of men dead, blood dripping all over the ground.
No one will defeat the Greeks whilst they march on to glory.

Rhys Keedwell (11)
YSGOL GYFUN Y CYMER RHONDDA, PORTH

TOM'S RUNAWAY

Tom looked back and saw that a man was following him so he began to run. The man followed. Tom took a shortcut down the alley but the man was already there with a knife in his hand. Tom didn't know what to do but stand there.

Dewi Evans (12)
YSGOL GYFUN Y CYMER RHONDDA, PORTH

THE ROOM

I walked up the horrid stairs stepping closer to the room. I looked around the dark landing, the walls covered with family pictures. My arm was on the door. 'Argh,' I screamed. 'Daniel, clean this room now!' I gave my son a Hoover and walked away smiling ear to ear.

Brioney Jones (13)
YSGOL GYFUN Y CYMER RHONDDA, PORTH

FOREST GIRL

One day a girl went into the forest. In the forest she wasn't looking where she was going and walked into a tree. She screamed to herself, 'That really hurt my head. I think I've broken my nose.'
She went to hospital and she never went to the forest again.

Nicola Lewis (13)
YSGOL GYFUN Y CYMER RHONDDA, PORTH

AN EMBARRASSING MOMENT

She walked through the school, all the kids pointed and laughed. She wondered why they were laughing at her and got embarrassed. She turned bright red and turned around to see what the fuss was about. 'Oh no! I have toilet paper trailing from my shoe.'

Katy Jones (13)
YSGOL GYFUN Y CYMER RHONDDA, PORTH

THE HAUNTED MANSION

One day a boy named Rhys journeyed into a big scary-looking house and in that scary-looking house there were cobwebs and old furniture. He had a look around and noticed a shadow behind him and it reached out and touched him. He ran for his life!

Curtis Griffiths (11)
YSGOL GYFUN Y CYMER RHONDDA, PORTH

A SECRET MISSION

He fell for a long time until he reached the bottom of
the well. There was a door, he opened it and found
a lost world full of magnificent treasure. Time was
running out, he had to go or he would fail his mission.
He hurried back to the headquarters.

Ethan Davies (12)
YSGOL GYFUN Y CYMER RHONDDA, PORTH

MY HAIR!

I walked into the bathroom, what a state on my hair.
I had a funny idea and thought, *what if it weren't there?*
A bald patch here, a bald patch there.
Oh this is a nightmare. Everywhere I go people stare
and say, 'Oh no! What happened to your hair?'

Kaisha Axford (11)
YSGOL GYFUN Y CYMER RHONDDA, PORTH

GEORGIA AND LUCKY'S LUCKY DAY!

Georgia had a horse for her tenth birthday. It was called Lucky. Lucky had never been in a show before. Lucky and Georgia entered in 'Best Looking Pony'. Lucky was black. Georgia and lucky won the competition. They won a red rosette and a big trophy. They were lucky!

Emily-Ann Greenslade (11)
YSGOL GYFUN Y CYMER RHONDDA, PORTH

DINNER LADY

Joanne worked in a fabulous diner called Joe's Diner.
It was great. She had a terrible husband, he was old
and never helped her.
One day she decided to run away. He was bullying her
and she was pregnant. She ran away and made her
own diner, Tami's Diner.

Sabrina Hosking (11)
YSGOL GYFUN Y CYMER RHONDDA, PORTH

INFORMATION

We hope you have enjoyed reading this book - and that you will continue to enjoy it in the coming years.

If you like reading and writing, drop us a line or give us a call and we'll send you a free information pack. Alternatively visit our website at www.youngwriters.co.uk

Write to:
Young Writers Information,
Remus House,
Coltsfoot Drive,
Peterborough,
PE2 9JX

Tel: (01733) 890066
Email: youngwriters@forwardpress.co.uk